Ju
F
Sp 3   Spector, Shoshannah.
          Five young heroes of
       Israel.

FIVE
YOUNG
HEROES
OF
ISRAEL

FIVE YOUNG HEROES

OF

ISRAEL

by SHOSHANNAH   SPECTOR

Illustrated by Aharon Shevo

SHENGOLD PUBLISHERS, INC.

New York

Library of Congress Catalog Card Number: 70-115117
Published by Shengold Publishers, Inc., New York
Copyright © 1970 by Shoshannah Spector
All rights reserved
Printed in the United States of America

*To the children
of the
State of Israel*

Overlooking the blue Sea of Galilee in the north of Israel there is a kibbutz. A kibbutz is a village where all the people live and work side by side as one large family on one big farm. Everyone shares in the chores, tilling the soil, harvesting the crops, caring for the chickens, sheep and cattle and tending the orchards where the good fruit grows for which Israel is known even in far-off countries.

On this kibbutz there are also many children. Our story is about five of them—Moshe, Hanna, Carmi, Meir and Shoshanna. They are good friends. They study together in the same schoolhouse; they work and play together almost all day long. They have known each other and lived near each other ever since they were born—all of eight years ago. That is why they are practically like brothers and sisters. They don't have the same parents, but they are so close to each

other's families that they even call each other's fathers and mothers by their first names—David, Miriam, Esther, Joel. This is not disrespectful—it's just the way things are done when you live in a kibbutz

Since the people in a kibbutz all live together like one large family, they also share the good things that happen— as well as the troubles.

The children help the grown-ups feed the animals and care for the gardens and the orchards. At harvest time they go out into the kibbutz fields along with the men and women to gather in the wheat and to take it to the barn where it is stored until it is ground into fine flour for bread.

Besides these big jobs, which all the people of the kibbutz do together, each of the five children in our story has his own special work which he does all alone.

Moshe's job is to tend the horses that work hard in the fields of the kibbutz all day. The minute school is over, Moshe hurries to the stable. He strokes the manes of Hayim, Yigal and Uzzi.

"How are you feeling? Are you very tired?" he asks the horses as he looks over their legs and hoofs. If he finds any little cuts or scratches, he washes them carefully and bandages them with strips of soft cloth.

"Don't I make a good doctor, Uzzi?" Moshe asks softly.

When Moshe grows up he wants to be a veterinarian, a doctor who treats not people but only animals and keeps them well and happy.

Uzzi gives a loud whinny.

"So you think I'm okay," says Moshe.

On days when there is no school, Moshe, his bright blue eyes shining, jumps on the back of Hayim, the friskiest horse in the stable, for a brisk romp, flying like the wind around the meadow until it is time for everyone to go to the dining hall for supper.

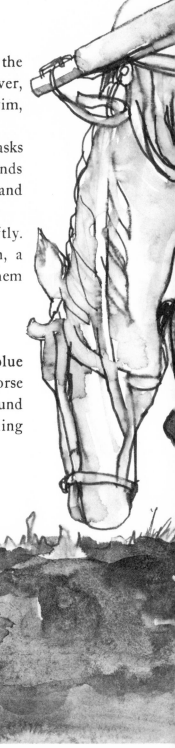

While Moshe is busy with the horses, black-eyed Hanna, her thick, black braids bouncing up and down, is off to the chicken coop, running and skipping all the way. In one hand she has a wooden bowl with chicken feed; her other hand is busy waving a big "Shalom" to everyone she passes. The baby chicks and the mother hens are waiting for her, bustling about, back and forth, cackling and pecking at the ground.

"Supper's ready," Hanna sings out. The chicks and the hens waddle up to her, cackling and chattering like so many gossiping old ladies.

"Hey, I want to hear the news, too," Hanna says and laughs. But the chickens are not listening. They are scrambling for the seeds Hanna has scattered on the ground for them.

"Well, it's no use talking to you when you are hungry," Hanna sighs. Very carefully, she gathers up the eggs the mother hens have laid. The mothers in the kibbutz kitchen need the eggs for baking the delicious kugels, cookies and other goodies everybody enjoys on the Sabbath.

"Thank you for the lovely eggs," Hanna whispers to the hens. "See you again tomorrow."

As soon as Carmi, the redhead, has finished his home-work, he runs to the cowshed to visit Sara, Rachel, Rebecca and Zilla, the cows of the kibbutz. Carmi picked their names himself—from the Bible stories Devora, the teacher, told the class in the little kibbutz schoolhouse. When the cows see Carmi coming, they start mooing so joyfully that you can hear them all over the kibbutz. Carmi thinks they must be very smart.

"I don't know how you do it," Carmi says as he holds out an armful of fresh straw to Zilla, "I mean, make sweet

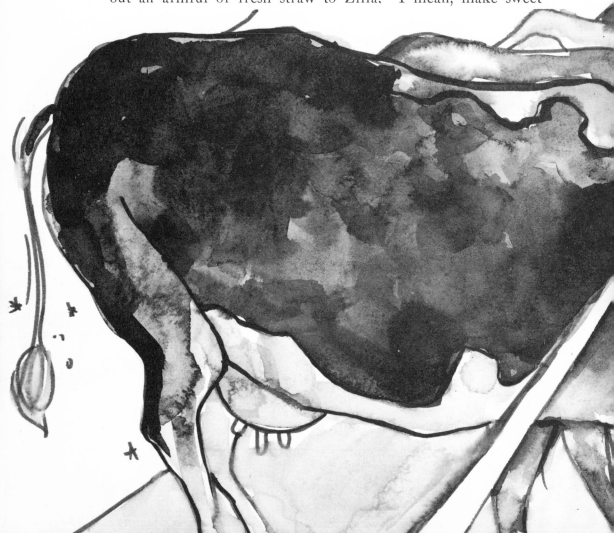

white milk out of all that dry, yellow straw you eat." He shakes his head. "Zilla, I just don't get it."

The friendly, speckled cows look at Carmi with their gentle, bulging eyes and chew their cud as if they were trying to think up a way of explaining it all to him. But they are too busy swinging their tails to chase the flies off their backs.

"Oh, never mind," Carmi says. "You can tell me some other time."

Meir, the most serious and grownup of the five, helps care for the kibbutz orchard, where the oranges grow. When the oranges are ripe, they turn a beautiful deep-yellow, orangey color and fill the air with a delicious sweet smell. That is the time when they have to be picked from their trees. Meir takes each ripe orange and wraps it carefully into thin, red paper.

"There you go," he whispers as he puts each fruit into
its own special place in the big wooden crates in which the
oranges will be taken to town to be sold. "Have a nice trip."
Meir is proud of his oranges, especially of those that go into the ice-cold drinks sold in sparkling bottles in stores all
over Israel.

Shoshanna, who is full of fun, loves her work in the vegetable garden. There, the green lettuce, the cucumbers, the peas, the carrots, the beans, the leafy spinach and the round, red tomatoes wait for Shoshanna to water them and to pull out the ugly weeds so they won't crowd out the healthy vegetables. "Who needs you?" Shoshanna scolds as she tears out a weed growing beside a plump cucumber.

There is a flower garden, too. The children are all very proud of their flowers which help make the kibbutz beautiful, almost like the garden of Eden in the Bible, Shoshanna thinks. Shoshanna is especially proud of the rose bushes where the birds make their nests. Shoshanna listens to the birds sing and makes up a song with words all her own which she teaches the rest of the children on long, quiet Sabbath afternoons.

The children have a share not only in the work of the kibbutz, but also in the fun. For instance, when a baby calf or lamb is born, the children choose the names for their new friends. When there is a holiday, the children help put up the holiday decorations of fragrant flowers and colorful vegetables in the kibbutz dining hall. And when the kibbutz gets visitors from far-off countries like England or the United States, it is the children who greet them and take them for a walk around the kibbutz. The children know everything there is to be known about the kibbutz and what goes on there.

At suppertime, the children sit with their fathers and mothers and talk about many things. Sometimes only the grownups talk and the children listen. The grownups talk about what is going on in the rest of Israel, outside the kibbutz. Sometimes they sound worried. Sometimes, big brothers and sisters leave the kibbutz and stay away for days. Or, in the middle of the night, a father will tiptoe into the room where his children are sleeping and kiss his little boy or girl. The next morning he is gone and one of the other men does his work in the kibbutz. Then, all of a sudden, he is back. The children know why all these things happen. Their fathers and their big brothers and sisters are taking turns guarding the borders of the country to keep Israel safe.

The children do a lot of thinking about their country. They don't like the fighting they hear about in the news. They want Israel and all the other countries around her to be friends, like everybody in their kibbutz. Then, they are sure, their fathers and mothers, and their big brothers and sisters, too, will stop worrying, and everybody will be happy.

One evening, just before the joyous holiday of Hanukkah, Moshe, Hanna, Carmi, Meir and Shoshanna got together and decided that they could make peace come faster by helping the grownups take care of Israel.

"After all," Meir, the most grownup of the five, said, "we're not babies any more. We're too big just to sit there and let the grownups do it all alone. If we are old enough to help take care of the horses and the chickens and the orchards of our kibbutz, we're old enough to help keep our country safe."

The next morning the five children went to school as usual, but they couldn't keep their minds on what Devora, their teacher, was saying.

"She teaches us how to read and write, and lots of other things," Hanna said to Shoshanna. "But why doesn't she teach us how to help our country? Isn't that just as important?"

The others agreed. Devora always told them stories about the heroes of the olden days. Now she had been telling them about the five brave brothers—the Maccabees—and their old father, Mattathias, who had saved the land of Israel from King Antiochus hundreds of years ago. She had told them

of the miracle that had come to pass. The small band of Maccabees had been able to drive out the wicked king and all his mighty army. Then, the five wonderful brothers had gone to reopen the Holy Temple in Jerusalem so that everyone might pray and give thanks to God for having helped the people of Israel win the war against the Greeks who had wanted to make them stop being Jews. The Maccabees had looked everywhere for oil pure enough to light the *menorah* of the Holy Temple, but there was no pure oil to be found. When they had just about given up, a little jug turned up which contained barely enough oil to burn for a single day. But the oil burned for eight whole days. And who had found that wonderful oil? Not one of the Maccabees, or one of the other Jewish soldiers, but a little boy. Well, if in those days a little boy could help a miracle to happen, why shouldn't the children of the kibbutz be able to help the grownups perform a miracle to make the fighting stop so that Israel and her neighbors could become good friends? Why, oh why, the children worried, didn't the teacher tell them how they could get the miracle started? One thing they knew: they would never be able to perform miracles by just sitting at home, or at school in the kibbutz. They would have to be right there, at the border, where the soldiers from their own kibbutz and from many other kibbutzim were standing guard.

That evening, after they had done their homework and finished their chores in the stable, in the chicken coop, in the cowshed and in the garden, Moshe, Hanna, Carmi, Meir and

Shoshanna got together under one of the orange trees in the orchard to decide what was to be done. The first thing they had to do, they all agreed, was to find a way of getting to the place where the soldiers were. And by bedtime, they had worked out a plan how to do just that.

They knew that, early the very next morning, the kibbutz truck would go down to the desert with milk and food for the soldiers in the army camp there. It would be perfect for what the children planned to do. While it would still be dark, they would climb into the kibbutz truck and hide behind the cans of milk and the crates of fruit and vegetables. The driver would never know that, along with the food, he would be taking five little Maccabees in the back of his truck down to the desert to help the soldiers there.

That night the children went to bed quickly. They wanted to be sure to wake up in time, before anyone would be able to keep them from carrying out their plan.

Moshe fell asleep at once. He had a dream. He dreamed he was already in the desert. He saw mountains of sand shaped like houses, gardens and forests. There was even a castle with tall towers, and a king and queen passing through the castle gate on two fine horses. Oh, and there was somebody else following right behind the king and queen. Why, it was Hanna!

"What are you doing here, Hanna?" Moshe cried out. "You're still supposed to be asleep in the kibbutz!"

But Hanna answered, "I'm not Hanna from the kibbutz."

"I'm Hanna from the Hanukkah story,
My seven sons gave their lives for God's glory.
They had made up their minds to refuse
Antiochus' command that they stop being Jews.
They decided they would rather die
Than disobey their God on high."

And then Hanna was gone. Moshe began to feel hot. "I'm burning up!" he said aloud. He looked for some shade, safe from the burning sun, but he could find no such place. He was thirsty, but there was no water anywhere. It was getting hotter all the time. The sun was blazing down on Moshe like a fire from a hot oven. Then, in the middle of the hot, dry desert, Moshe saw a tall tree, with plenty of leaves to give him shelter from the burning sun. He began to run toward the tree. He ran and ran, but the tree was no closer. He got tired and slowed down to a walk, but the tree stayed as far away from him as before. He walked for four days and nights. On the fifth day he saw that the tree was right in front of him. Moshe stretched out his hand to touch the tree, but it was not a tree at all— only a rock shaped like a tree. Moshe was ready to cry.

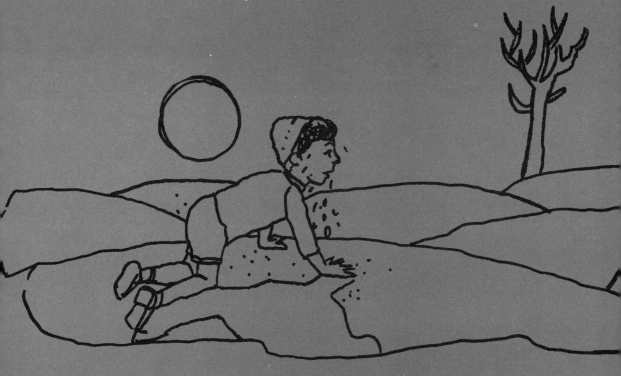

But what was that behind the rock? A man? Who could that man be? Moshe wondered. He looked closer. It was his friend, Carrot-top Carmi! Only now Carmi wasn't wearing the blue overalls he usually wore when he went to visit the cows in the kibbutz. He was dressed like a king, with a crown on his head. He was standing in front of a statue that had the face of a bird, and he kept bowing down to it.

"Hey, Carmi, where did you get that crown?" Moshe shouted," and why are you bowing down to that silly bird?"

"How dare you call me Carmi?" Carmi shouted back.

"I'm King Antiochus, the Greek,
You'd better listen when I speak,
And this is not a silly bird,
So listen and don't say a word.

"This, my boy, is my royal command.
Let every person understand:
I bow to this bird. You must bow to it, too.
That's what I expect of every Jew."

Moshe couldn't believe his ears.

"Carmi, what's the matter with you?" he cried. "Jews pray to God, not to idols."

"I'm King Antiochus," Carmi repeated.

"Stop it, Carmi!" Moshe yelled. He was almost crying. "You're *not* a wicked king! You're Carmi, the redhead from the kibbutz!"

But Carmi didn't answer. In fact, he was gone. In his place there was an old man, dressed in white, with a long, white beard. When the old man came closer, Moshe saw that it was Meir, who worked in the kibbutz orchard.

"What are you doing here, Meir?" Moshe asked him. "We were supposed to meet near the kibbutz truck—not here, in the middle of nowhere."

"What's a kibbutz truck?" Meir demanded, "and who told you my name's Meir?"

"Well, what is your name, then?" Moshe asked.
"I'm Mattathias, the priest of old,
The father of the Maccabees bold,
I'm getting together a brave, strong band
To come to the aid of our people and land.

"Let Israel's soldiers brave arise
And drive off our enemies.
Let those who want our country free
Pray to the Lord and come to me."
With that, Meir spread out his arms, raised his head
and shouted:
"Let all those who love God come to me!"
Suddenly, there were all the children of the kibbutz, rush-
ing up to Meir. Moshe was running and shouting along with
the rest. He was carrying a shining shield in one hand and a
spear in the other. Just as he was about to hurl his spear at

the enemy, he heard a voice whispering:

"Moshe! Moshe! It's time to get up! The kids are waiting! It'll be light soon! We've got to get to the truck before anybody catches us."

Moshe reached for his shining shield, but all he found in his hand was a corner of his woolen blanket. And he wasn't in the desert, but in his own bed.

Moshe jumped out of bed. In the dark, he reached for the chair next to his bed and grabbed the pants and the shirt he had worn the day before. Quickly, he slipped into his clothes. Then, he ran to the sink, splashed some water on his face and rubbed his eyes. It was too dark—and also too late —to look for his comb, so Moshe just ran his fingers through his hair. And before you could count to ten, Moshe was outside, running toward the kibbutz truck. He found Hanna, Carmi, Meir and Shoshanna already there waiting for him.

"Whew!" Meir gave a low whistle. "I thought you'd never make it, Moshe. C'mon, gang, let's get going."

Moshe, Hanna, Carmi, Meir and Shoshanna climbed into the back of the kibbutz truck and hid behind a stack of crates.

It was still dark. The children sat quietly in the back of the truck. From time to time, they looked around to see whether everybody else was really there. They felt as if they were still dreaming. But then they heard two men get into the truck up front. With a jolt, the truck began to move, and before long the children were wide awake. A banana from one of the fruit baskets fell into Shoshanna's lap. Shoshanna giggled.

"Quiet!" Meir hissed. "They'll hear us."

The driver up front was singing *Yerushalayim shel Zahav,* the song about the beautiful, golden city of Jerusalem which the children all knew and loved. The other man was singing along. But the children couldn't join in because they were not really supposed to be in the truck and didn't want to be found

out after all the trouble they had gone through. The man sitting next to the driver, the children knew, was a soldier with a rifle in his hand, who had come along to help in case anything went wrong on the trip through the desert.

The children sat in the truck without daring to move. It was a bumpy ride.

"I'm stiff," Carmi grumbled.

"So am I," said Moshe.

"Quiet, everybody!" said Meir.

After what seemed hours, the children heard the soldier say to the driver:

"We should be there in another half-hour's time. We'll unload the food from the truck and carry it into the camp."

It was getting lighter outside. The children started talking to each other in sign language.

"Now does everybody remember what we're going to do?" Meir whispered.

The children hadn't forgotten. This was their plan:

When the truck would stop, they would wait, huddled in a corner of the truck, until the two men had gone with the first load of food. Then, the children would jump off the truck, one at a time. That way, they wouldn't be making too much noise. By the time the men would be back for the second load of food, all the children would be out of the truck and hiding in the sand or behind a rock. When the men would have walked away from the truck with the last load of food, the children would all come out from their hiding places and walk toward the camp. Once they were at the camp, they were sure, nobody would be able to make them go back to the kibbutz.

The truck came to a stop. The children heard the driver and the soldier get off. As soon as the two men had walked away with the first load of food, the five children crept out from behind the crates and the milk containers. Hanna jumped first. Shoshanna came next. A few minutes later, Moshe jumped. Carmi followed. The last to leave the truck was Meir. By the time the two men had returned for the second load of food, the children were all out of the truck and well hidden from view.

When the men had gone with the very last load of food, Meir crept out from behind the rock where he had been hiding.

"Let's go," he said in a hoarse voice just loud enough for the others to hear.

Four heads appeared from four different hiding places in the cold, bleak desert.

"Moshe?" Meir asked.

"Here," Moshe replied and dusted the sand from his pants.

"Hanna?" Meir asked next.

"H--here," Hanna said. "B--rr, it's c--c-cold."

"Carmi?" Meir called.

"Here," Carmi answered and shook the sand out of his red hair.

"Shoshanna?"

"Here," said Shoshanna and giggled. "This is fun."

"The men walked down that way," Meir said, pointing with his finger. "See the footprints?"

All together, the five children followed the footprints, which led straight to the army camp.

Meanwhile, back on the kibbutz, the new day was just about to begin. The fathers and mothers were up and about, getting ready for the day's work. In the kibbutz kitchen, Meir's father was stirring some hot cereal in a huge kettle for breakfast.

Just then, Meir's mother rushed into the kitchen.

"Where's Meir?" she cried. "He's not in his bed! Is he with you?"

Meir's father stopped stirring the cereal.

"So he's not in his bed? He's probably gone off to the schoolhouse to get the chalk and the paper ready for the teacher. Wait, I'll go see."

Just as Meir's father went out through the kitchen door, Hanna's mother ran toward him.

"Hanna's gone!" she said. "I went to wake her up but she wasn't in her bed."

Carmi's father walked in. "Has any one seen Carmi?" he asked.

Moshe's grandmother, still in her bathrobe, was there, too.

"Something's wrong, very wrong! I just know it!" She began to cry. "We've been looking everywhere for Moshe and we can't find him."

Shoshanna's father and mother appeared. They looked worried.

"So you can't find your children, either?" Shoshanna's mother asked the other parents. "Well, no use just standing here. Let's look around the kibbutz. They can't just have disappeared. They have to be someplace."

The other parents followed Shoshanna's mother to the schoolhouse. From there, they went to the cowshed. Next, they searched the stable and the chicken coop. Moshe's father was looking in the orchard.

At first, the fathers were just angry. They all agreed that they would punish their children so that they would never, never run away again.

"Moshe won't be allowed to feed the horses for a whole month," Moshe's father said.

"And I won't let Hanna go to the chicken coop after school," said Hanna's father.

Carmi's father banged his fist on the dining room table. "He'll be sorry all right. He won't get to see the new baby calf in the cowshed till next week."

The mothers of the children weren't even thinking about punishment. They were crying.

"What could have happened to them?" they asked each other.

"Where do you think they could have gone?" the fathers asked Devora, the teacher.

Devora was worried, too. She remembered that Moshe, Hanna, Carmi, Meir and Shoshanna had been unusually quiet lately. They had sat in class without saying a word or even asking questions. But as soon as the bell rang, they had jumped from their seats and rushed out of the schoolhouse before all the others.

"You know, I heard them talking about the Maccabees just yesterday," said Devora.

"Moshe was all excited about King Antiochus," Moshe's mother remembered.

"Meir was talking about Hanukkah all during supper." Meir mother said. "And then he went off to bed. All by himself. No one had to tell him what the time was."

Hanna's mother noded excitedly. "My Hanna went to sleep so early I was worried she might be sick."

"Carmi was ready for bed at seven," Carmi's mother said, "and he never wants to go to bed."

"Shoshanna hardly said anything last night," Shoshanna's mother recalled. "And you know what a chatterbox she usually is."

The other people of the kibbutz began to drift into the dining hall in small groups. One of the older men was holding a small transistor radio in his hand.

"Quiet, everybody!" he said. "There's news!"

Everybody stopped talking. In Israel, people always stop talking while the news comes over the radio. Even the parents of the five missing children stopped to listen to the news.

"And now," the announcer was saying, "for a most unusual story. Early this morning five children—three boys and two girls—marched into an army camp and asked to see the captain.

" 'What do you want?' the captain asked them.

" 'We want to help you keep our country safe,' one of the boys answered.

"The children said that at the kibbutz where they lived, near the Sea of Galilee, they did everything the grownups did —feed the animals, care for the orchards and harvest the crops. So, they said, if they could help the grownups take care of the kibbutz, they were also old enough to help take care of their country.

"The captain thought for a while and then explained to the children that the soldiers could keep the country safe only if they knew that there were enough people left in the kibbutz to take care of the fields and the animals. After all, the country needs the milk, the vegetables, the fruit and the grain that come from the kibbutz. The captain gave the children a good breakfast of bread, olives, cheese and hot chocolate. By now, they ought to be on their way back to their kibbutz."

A few hours later, a jeep pulled up at the kibbutz gate, with an officer in the driver's seat and five very tired youngsters sitting beside and behind the driver. Practically everyone of the kibbutz, from the youngest to the oldest, had turned out to welcome the children back. The fathers and mothers

were so happy to see their little heroes safe and sound that they forgot about punishing them. They hugged and kissed them, but they cried a little, too, because they were proud of them for having wanted so much to help their country.

The next day was the first night of Hanukkah. That evening, everybody in the kibbutz gathered in the dining hall for the kindling of the first Hanukkah light on the *menorah*. Everybody joined in the Hanukkah songs, played game after game of *draydel* for sweet, wrinkly raisins and ate dozens of golden brown, delicious fried *latkes*. And then everybody danced until it was almost morning.

Of course, each child got a Hanukkah surprise. When Moshe opened his package, he found a brush to smooth the coats of the horses. Hanna's gift was a charm bracelet, with five red and yellow chicks. Carmi got a milk container, like those in the cowshed, except that it was shiny and very much smaller. A tag on the container said that it was a gift from his friends Sara, Rebecca, Rachel and Zilla, the cows. Meir got a picture book about oranges, lemons and grapefruits. Shoshanna's present was a little green spade and rake to use in the vegetable garden.

After the children had thanked their parents for their gifts, Meir's father got up from his seat, walked up to the big *menorah* and made a speech of his own.

"I think we ought to thank our children," he said. "They gave us and our kibbutz the most wonderful Hanukkah gift of all—the feeling that we can depend on them to grow into fine, brave young men and women, who love not only their families and their kibbutz but also their country—like the Maccabees of long ago."

TEMPLE ISRAEL LIBRARY

Temple Israel

Minneapolis, Minnesota

In Honor of the Bar Mitzvah of
DAVID A. OSTROV
by
Dr. and Mrs. Charles S. Ostrov